Emily's Tiger

Dedicated to Hannah, love from Mimi xx — M. L.

Barefoot Books
124 Walcot Street
Bath BA1 5BG

First published in Great Britain in 2008 by Barefoot Books, Ltd

This book has been printed on 100% acid-free paper

Graphic design by Judy Linard, London
Colour separation by Grafiscan, Verona
Printed and bound in Singapore by Tien Wah Press Pte Ltd

This book was typeset in Zemke Hand ITC 24 and 65 on 33 point
The illustrations were prepared in acrylics and collage

Hardback ISBN 978-1-84686-137-6

British Cataloguing-in-Publication Data:
a catalogue record for this book is available from the British Library

3 5 7 9 8 6 4 2

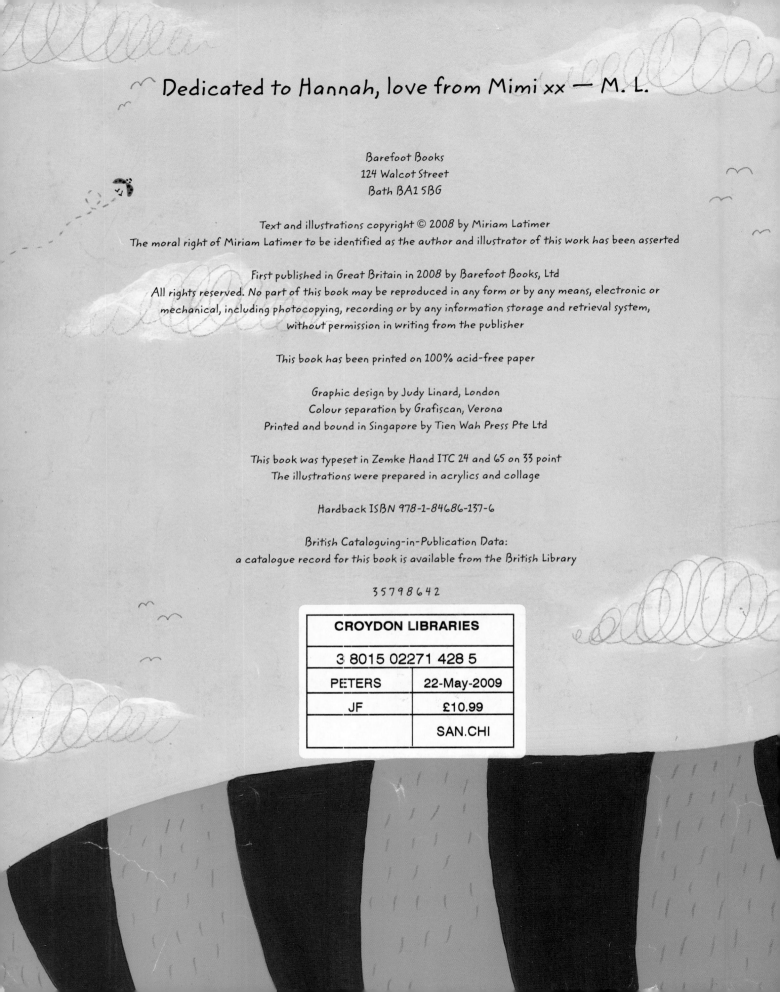

Emily's Tiger

Miriam Latimer

Barefoot Books
Celebrating Art and Story

'I don't want my hair cut,'
Emily pouted.

'Emily, please sit down,'
Mum sighed.

. . . she gave her loudest tiger ROAR!
'Not again!' Mum groaned.
'Come here, you rascal!'
Emily bounded round the room,
and bounced out of the window.

'Oh, Emily,' Mum sighed again.
'What are we going to do with you?'

Later, at Evie's party, the clown announced, 'I need an assistant.'

'Me!' squealed Emily.

'I choose Evie, the birthday girl,'
said the clown.

'But I want to be the helper!'
growled Emily.

The clown shook his head.
        Emily stamped her foot and gave
            a huge . . .

ROAR!

Soon Evie's party was in chaos.

'Oh, Emily,' sighed Dad when he came to take her home. 'What are we going to do with you?'

At supper time, Dad tried to persuade
Emily to eat some carrots.

'I don't like carrots!' Emily snapped, and swishing her long curly tail, she swiped her plate right up into the air.

'Oh, Emily!' groaned Mum. Just then, the doorbell rang.

'Hello, I'm here!' sang Granny as she pranced through the door. 'Gollygumdrops, it looks like a zoo in here. What's been going on?'

'I got upset, Granny. I don't like carrots.' Emily hung her head.

'Oh, Emily,' smiled Granny, 'What are we going to do with you? I know, let's go upstairs.'

'I want to share a secret with you,'
whispered Granny. She turned away
and when she looked back, Granny
gave a loud tiger . . .

ROAR!

'Eeek!' Emily jumped back in surprise.

'No need to be scared, pumpkin,' Granny assured her. 'I only turn into a tiger when I want to. That way, I can turn myself into a happy tiger instead of an angry one. And happy tigers have much more fun.'

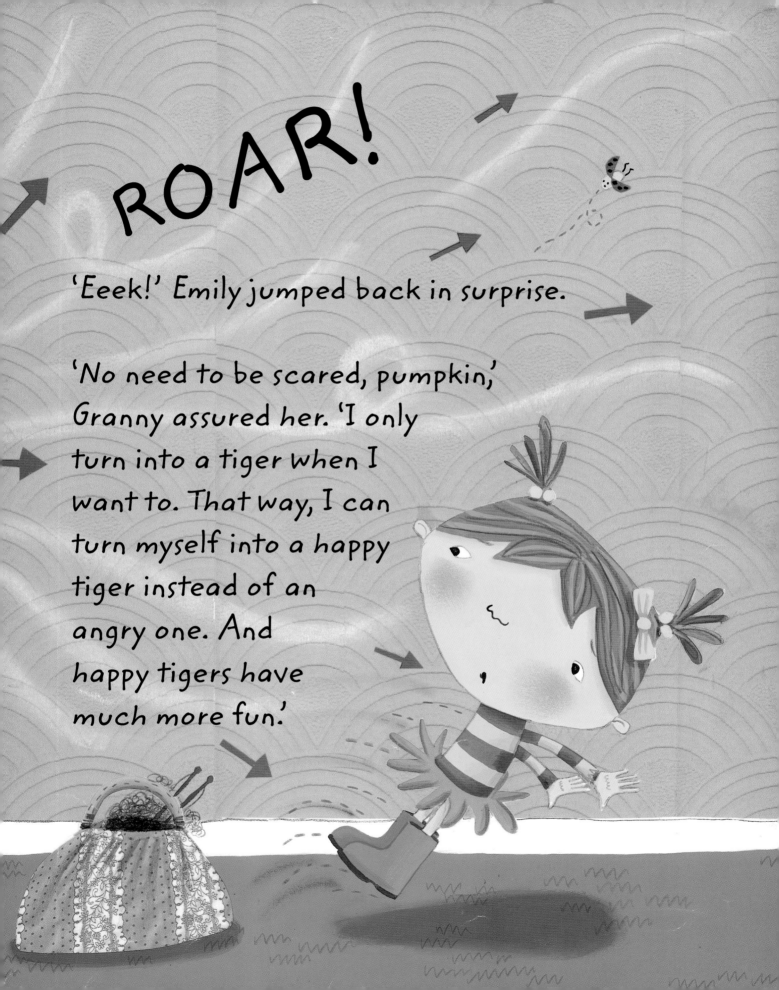

That night, Emily dreamt about
being a tiger with Granny.

Together, they leapt all the way along the roofs of the cars that were parked in Emily's street.

'Higher?' asked Granny. Emily nodded, and they leapt all the way along the roofs of the houses.

'Higher?' asked Granny. Emily nodded, and Granny leapt right over the moon. Emily didn't dare follow her there.

'How did you do that?' she said.

'You'll learn,' Granny smiled.

'Have you brushed your teeth yet?'
Mum asked Emily in the morning.
'I hate brushing my teeth!'
said Emily.
'I love brushing mine,'
whispered Granny.

Emily decided to brush
her teeth to shine just
like Granny's.

After school, Granny and Emily went to the park. Emily spotted Dylan Jones making a camp.

'Can I help?' asked Emily.

But as she peeped inside Dylan's tent he climbed on to her bike and began riding it round the park.

'Hey, give it back!' shouted Emily and she crouched down, ready to pounce.

Then she glimpsed over at Granny. Her big paws were wrapped round a book. She looked very relaxed.

Emily decided to relax, just like Granny.
'Yippee!' Dylan whooped as he pedalled
past. Emily ignored him.

Dylan tried riding with no hands. He lost
his balance and fell off.

'Wahhh!' he yelled.

Emily helped Dylan to pick himself up.
'Are you OK?'
she asked.

Granny grinned
and gave Emily
a big thumbs up.

At supper time, Emily ate all of her carrots — just like Granny.

She helped Dad wash up, and she brushed
her teeth without even the slightest growl.

Later on, there was a rat-tat-tat-tat on Emily's bedroom door.

'Psst!' whispered Granny. 'Follow me.' And they crept outside.

'Now for the fun bit,' said Granny.
'Come on, Emily!' she called as she
fearlessly hurdled the garden fence.
She showed Emily how to soar
over hedges, scale walls
and climb trees.

'Happy tiger or angry tiger?'
asked Granny.

'Happy tiger!' cried Emily,
and then she jumped right
over the moon.

Barefoot Books
Celebrating Art and Story

At Barefoot Books, we celebrate art and story that opens
the hearts and minds of children from all walks of life, inspiring
them to read deeper, search further, and explore their own creative gifts.
Taking our inspiration from many different cultures, we focus on themes that
encourage independence of spirit, enthusiasm for learning, and sharing of
the world's diversity. Interactive, playful and beautiful, our products
combine the best of the present with the best of the past
to educate our children as the caretakers of tomorrow.

Live Barefoot!
Join us at www.barefootbooks.com